Roscoe the Raccoon

Papa tells Roscoe to manage his behavior.

Papa takes Roscoe to see Olivia Owl.

Papa asks Olivia to help Roscoe.

Roscoe says, "Sometimes I forget
and don't do what I need to."

Clarence Coyote teases Roscoe.

"Lots of interesting things are out there,"
says Clarence.

Roscoe dreams about treasures.

Olivia swoops down.

Olivia asks, "Are you doing your BEST?"

Roscoe knows how to TEAM.

Roscoe whistles a tune.

ISBN-13: 978-0-87822-579-8
ISBN-10: 0-87822-579-X

90000

EAN

9 780878 225798